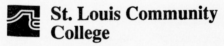

AS THE STORY
WAS TOLD

Other Works by Samuel Beckett

Novels:

MURPHY

WATT

FIRST LOVE

MERCIER AND CAMIER

MOLLOY

MALONE DIES

THE UNNAMABLE

HOW IT IS

COMPANY

ILL SEEN ILL SAID

WORSTWORD HO

Short Prose:

MORE PRICKS THAN KICKS

FOUR NOVELLAS

TEXTS FOR NOTHING

ALL STRANGE AWAY

IMAGINATION DEAD IMAGINE

NO'S KNIFE

SIX RESIDUA

FOR TO END YET AGAIN

   and other Fizzles

COLLECTED SHORTER PROSE

   1945-1980

STIRRINGS STILL

Poems:

AN ANTHOLOGY OF MEXICAN POETRY (translation)

ZONE (translation)

COLLECTED POEMS 1930-1978

Criticism:

PROUST and THREE DIALOGUES WITH GEORGES DUTHUIT

DISJECTA

Plays:

COME AND GO

THE OLD TUNE (translation in PINGET PLAYS VOLUME I

AS THE
STORY WAS TOLD

Uncollected and Late Prose

Samuel Beckett

JOHN CALDER · LONDON
RIVERRUN PRESS · NEW YORK

First published in Great Britain in 1990 by
John Calder (Publishers) Ltd
9-15 Neal Street, London WC2H 9TU

and in the United States of America in 1990 by
Riverrun Press Inc
1170 Broadway, New York, NY 10001

British Library Cataloguing in Publication Data
Beckett, Samuel, *1906-1989*
    As the story was told: uncollected and late prose.
    I. Title
    828.91208

    ISBN 0-7145-4113-3

Library of Congress Cataloging in Publication Data
Beckett, Samuel, 1906-1989
    As the story was told: uncollected and late prose/Samuel Beckett.
        p. cm   90-8136
    ISBN 0-7145-4113-3 : $19.95   CIP
    I. Title.
    PR 6003.   E282A9   1990
    848'.91409—dc 20

Typeset in 16½ point Garamond by Maggie Spooner Typesetting, London.
Printed and bound in Great Britain by Southampton Book Co, Southampton.

CONTENTS

PREFACE

This volume contains those texts of Samuel Beckett that have not been published in the United Kingdom in a trade edition, together with others that have been collected in Britain, but not in the United States of America, where this volume will be simultaneously published.

As the Story was Told is in five sections. Part I contains a text written in 1946 for Radio Éireann, as is explained in Dougald McMillan's introductory note. Part II contains two texts which were early exercises for later works: *The Image* was published in the review *X*, edited by Mary Hutchinson and Sonia Orwell, of which only one issue appeared around 1962, but it was written in the fifties and is an *esquisse* for *How It Is*; *All Strange Away* is an early version of *Imagination Dead Imagine* and first appeared ten years after it in 1976 in a limited edition published in New York by Gotham Book Mart, illustrated by Edward Gorey, before British publication in 1978.

Part III contains four short texts

that were included in the *Collected Shorter Prose 1945-1980*, a volume that never appeared in the United States of America. Of these *Heard in the Dark 1* and *2* are early versions of *Company*. *neither* was written for the American composer Morton Feldman, since deceased, and receives its world première in 1990 in Amsterdam. It was inadvertantly omitted from the *Shorter Prose* after the Author asked that it should not be included in the *Collected Poems*, of which an updated edition containing late poems will appear in 1991.

Stirrings Still appeared on the last day of 1988 in a *de luxe* edition, limited to two hundred copies, illustrated and signed by Louis le Brocquy and the Author. *What is the word* is Beckett's final literary utterance and is collected here for the first time.

The sad death of Samuel Beckett just before Christmas 1989 makes this final volume of prose a memorial. The publishers wish to record their deep affection for an author whose greatness is now recognised and with whom they enjoyed a personal and professional relationship for more than thirty-five years.

THE PUBLISHERS

PART I

THE CAPITAL
OF THE RUINS

INTRODUCTION

The following script was read by
Beckett on Radio Éireann on 10 June,
1946. It grew out of Beckett's
experience in the town of Saint-Lô
on the Normandy coast and in the
Irish Red Cross Hospital there where
he served as an interpreter and store
keeper from August 1945 to January
1946. After leaving Paris in 1942
where his services to the resistance

13

won him the *Croix de Guerre*, he passed the remainder of the war in hiding in Roussillon. When France was liberated, he returned to Ireland but in order to be able to return to France and ultimately to his remaining friends and pre-war apartment in Paris, he volunteered for service with the Irish Red Cross in Normandy. His experience there was in many ways the culmination of his engagement in World War II. (He spoke later of his final duty at the Hospital — finding a way to exterminate the rats which particularly threatened the maternity and Children's wards — as his last personal act of war.)

The title of the script is borrowed

14

from the people of Saint-Lô who had prepared a booklet of photographs entitled *Saint-Lô, Capital des Ruines, 5 et 7 Juin, 1944* which showed the town before the night it was bombed and afterwards.

The practical occasion of the radio script was public Dublin disparagement of the equipment and conditions of the Hospital implying criticism of the French for not making better provision. Like his earlier *Che scigura* and 'Censorship in the Sarostat' written while at Trinity College, *The Capital of the Ruins* is a rare piece of polemic attempting to correct Irish parochialism. But it is also an even more rare direct personal statement

15

about the significance of his experience in war-ravaged France.

Dougald McMillan

THE CAPITAL
OF THE RUINS

On what a year ago was a grass slope,
lying in the angle that the Vire and
Bayeux roads make as they unite at
the entrance of the town, opposite
what remains of the second most
important stud-farm in France, a
general hospital now stands. It is
the Hospital of the Irish Red Cross
in Saint-Lô, or, as the Laudiniens

17

themselves say, the Irish Hospital. The buildings consist of some prefabricated wooden huts. They are superior, generally speaking, to those so scantily available for the wealthier, the better-connected, the astuter or the more fragrantly deserving of the bombed-out. Their finish, as well without as within, is the best that their priority can command. They are lined with glass-wool and panelled in isorel, a strange substance of which there are only very limited supplies available. There is real glass in the windows. The consequent atmosphere is that of brightness and airiness so comforting to sick people, and to weary staffs. The floors, there where the exigencies of hygiene are greatest, are covered with linoleum. There was not enough linoleum left in France to do more than this. The walls and ceiling of the operating theatre are sheeted in aluminium of aeronautic origin, a decorative and practical solution to an old problem and a pleasant variation on the sword and ploughshare metamorphosis. A system of covered ways connects the kitchen with refectories and wards. The supply of electric current, for purposes both of heat and of power, leaves nothing to be desired, though painstakingly anonymous attempts were made, in this country, as recently I think as last winter, to prove the contrary. The hospital is centrally heated throughout, by means of coke. The medical, scientific, nursing and secretarial staffs are Irish, the instruments and furniture (including of course beds and bedding), the drugs and food, are supplied by the Society. I think I am right in saying that the number of in-patients (mixed) is in the neighbourhood of ninety. As for the others, it is a regular thing, according to recent reports, for as many as two hundred to be seen in the out-patients department in a day. Among such ambulant cases a large number are suffering from scabies and other diseases of the skin, the result no doubt of malnutrition or an ill-advised diet. Accident cases are frequent. Masonry falls when least expected, children play with detonators and demining continues. The laboratory, magnificently equipped, bids well to become the official laboratory for the department, if not of an even wider area. Considerable work has already been done in the analysis of local waters.

These few facts, chosen not quite at random, are no doubt familiar already to those at all interested in the subject, and perhaps even to those of you listening to me now. They may not appear the most immediately instructive. That the operating-theatre should be sheeted with an expensive metal, or the floor of the labour room covered with linoleum, can hardly be expected to interest those accustomed to such conditions as the *sine qua non* of reputable obstetrical and surgical statistics. These are the sensible people who would rather have news of the Norman's semi-circular canals or resistance to sulphur than of his attitude to the Irish bringing gifts, who would prefer the history of our difficulties with an unfamiliar pharmacopia and system of mensuration to the story of our dealings with the rare and famous ways of spirit that are the French ways. And yet the

22

whole enterprise turned from the beginning on the establishing of a relation in the light of which the therapeutic relation faded to the merest of pretexts.

What was important was not our having penicillin when they had none, nor the unregarding munificence of the French Ministry of Reconstruction (as it was then called), but the occasional glimpse obtained, by us in them and, who knows, by them in us (for they are an imaginative people), of that smile at the human conditions as little to be extinguished by bombs as to be broadened by the elixirs of Burroughs and Welcome, — the smile deriding, among other things,

23

the having and the not having, the giving and the taking, sickness and health.

It would not be seemly, in a retiring and indeed retired store-keeper, to describe the obstacles encountered in this connection, and the forms, often grotesque, devised for them by the combined energies of the home and visiting temperaments. It must be supposed that they were not insurmountable, since they have long ceased to be of much account. When I reflect now on the recurrent problems of what, with all proper modesty, might be called the heroic period, on one in particular so arduous and elusive that it literally

24

ceased to be formulable, I suspect that our pains were those inherent in the simple and necessary and yet so unattainable proposition that their way of being we, was not our way and that our way of being they, was not their way. It is only fair to say that many of us had never been abroad before.

Saint-Lô was bombed out of existence in one night. German prisoners of war, and casual labourers attracted by the relative food-plenty, but soon discouraged by housing conditions, continue, two years after the liberation, to clear away the debris, literally by hand. Their spirit has yet to learn the blessings of

Gallup and their flesh the benefits of the bulldozer. One may thus be excused if one questions the opinion generally received, that ten years will be sufficient for the total reconstruction of Saint-Lô. But no matter what period of time must still be endured, before the town begins to resemble the pleasant and prosperous administrative and agricultural centre that it was, the hospital of wooden huts in its gardens between the Vire and Bayeux roads will continue to discharge its function, and its cures. 'Provisional' is not the term it was, in this universe become provisional. It will continue to discharge its function long after the Irish are gone and their

26

names forgotten. But I think that to the end of its hospital days it will be called the Irish Hospital, and after that the huts, when they have been turned into dwellings, the Irish huts. I mention this possibility, in the hope that it will give general satisfaction. And having done so I may perhaps venture to mention another, more remote but perhaps of greater import in certain quarters, I mean the possibility that some of those who were in Saint-Lô will come home realising that they got at least as good as they gave, that they got indeed what they could hardly give, a vision and sense of a time-honoured conception of humanity in ruins, and perhaps even an inkling of the terms in which our condition is to be thought again. These will have been in France.

PART II

THE IMAGE

ALL STRANGE AWAY

THE IMAGE

My tongue fills my mouth with mud a
last resource takes it in and turns the
mud around in the mouth question
if swallowed would it nourish and
opening up of vistas without having
to swallow often they are not bad
moments to spend everything there
rosy in the mud the tongue lolls out
again and what are the hands at all this
time one must always try and see what

the hands are at well the left as we
have seen still clutches the sack and
the right well the right after a
moment at the end of its arm full
stretch in the axis of the clavicule as it
might be said or rather opening and
closing in the mud opening and
closing it's another of my resources
this little movement helps me I don't
know why I have little tricks like
that which are a good resource even
following the walls under the chang-
ing sky I should be shrewder it can't
be far a bare yard but it feels far it will
go some day by itself on its four
fingers including the thumb because
one is missing not the thumb it will
leave me I can see it how it throws its

four fingers forward like grapnells
the ends sink pull and so with little
horizontal hoists it moves away that's
what I like to proceed like that little
by little and the legs what are the legs
doing oh the legs and the eyes what
are the eyes doing closed no doubt no
since suddenly there in the mud I see
me I say me as I say I as I will say he
because it amuses me I look to me
about sixteen and to complete the
happiness glorious weather egg-blue
sky and scamper of little clouds I turn
my back and the girl too whom I hold
by the hand the arse which if I may
judge from the flowers that deck the
emerald grass we are in the month of
April or in May I don't know from

where and with what pleasure I
received this knowledge of flowers
and seasons I received it somehow it
must be judged by certain accessories
white rails and grandstand of
marvellous red we are on a racecourse
head thrown back gazing I imagine
straight ahead still as statues save
only the swinging arms with hands
clasped in my free hand or left an
undefinable object and consequently
in her right the extremity of a short
lease connecting her to an ash-grey
terrier of fair size askew on its
hunkers its head sunk stillness of
those hands and the corresponding
arms question why a leash in this
immensity of verdure and emergence

little by little of grey and white spots
to which I do not hesitate to give the
names of lambs among their dams I
don't know from where I received
this knowledge of animals I received
it somehow it all happened one day
that I knew how to name four or five
dogs of totally different breeds I saw
them trying above all not to
understand on the horizon four or
five miles off as the crow flies the
bluish bulk of a mountain of modest
elevation our heads overtop the crest
as of a single and same impulse or as
if synchronised we let go our hands
and turn about I dextrogyre she
sinistro she transfers the lease to her
left hand and I the same instant to my

right the object now a little pale grey
brick-shaped package perhaps of
sandwiches caused no doubt by being
able to hold hands once again the
arms swing the dog has not moved I
have the absurd impression we are
looking at me I pull in my tongue
close my mouth and smile seen full
face the girl is less hideous it's not
with her I am concerned me pale
brush-cut hair red pudding face with
pimples protruding belly gaping fly
spindle legs sagging knocking at the
knees wide straddle for greater
stability feet splayed one hundred
and thirty-five degrees fatuous half-
smile to posterior horizon figuring
the beginning of life green tweeds

yellow boots cowslip or suchlike in the buttonhole again about turn inward so as to bring us fleetingly not back to back but face to face at ninety degrees mingling of hands swinging of arms stillness of dog the rump I have three two one left right off we go chins up arms swinging the dog follows head sunk tail on balls no reference to us it had the same motion at the same instant as Malebranche less the rosy hue the humanities I had if it stops to piss it will piss without stopping I want to shout plant her there and run open your veins three hours of measured steps and there we are on the summit the dog askew on its hunkers in the heather it lowers its snout to its penis black and pink from much licking we on the contrary again about turn introrse transfer of hands swinging of arms silent relishing of sea and isles heads pivoting as one to the city fumes silent location of the tops of monuments heads back front as if connected patch of fog and suddenly we are eating sandwiches alternate bites each their own while exchanging endearments my sweet girl she bites I swallow we don't yet coo with our bills full my darling girl I bite she swallows my darling boy she bites I swallow brief fog and there we are again dwindling again across the pastures hand in hand arms swinging

heads high towards the heights
smaller and smaller I no longer see
the dog no longer us the scene is shut
of us some animals still the sheep like
granite outcrops horse I hadn't seen
standing motionless back bent head
animals know blue and white of sky
April morning in the mud it's over
it's done I've had the image the scene
is empty a few animals still then goes
out no more blue I stay there over
there on the right in the mud the
hands opens and closes that helps me
it's going let it go I realise I'm still
smiling there's been no sense in that
for a long time now my tongue
comes out again lolls in the mud I
stay there no more thirst the tongue

goes in the mouth closes it must be a straight line now it's over it's finished I've had the image.

ALL STRANGE AWAY

Imagination dead imagine. A place, that again. Never another question. A place, then someone in it, that again. Crawl out of the frowsy deathbed and drag it to a place to die in. Out of the door and down the road in the old hat and coat like after the war, no, not that again. Five foot square, six high, no way in, none out, try for him there. Stool, bare walls when the light comes

on, women's faces on the walls when
the light comes on. In a corner when
the light comes on tattered syntaxes of
Jolly and Draeger Praeger Draeger,
all right. Light off and let him be, on
the stool, talking to himself in the last
person, murmuring, no sound, Now
where is he, no, Now he is here.
Sitting, standing, walking, kneeling,
crawling, lying, creeping, in the dark
and in the light, try all. Imagine light.
Imagine light. No visible source, glare
at full, spread all over, no shadow, all
six planes shining the same, slow on,
ten seconds on earth to full, same off,
try that. Still his crown touches the
ceiling, moving not, say a lifetime of
walking bowed and full height when

42

brought to a stand. It goes out, no matter, start again, another place, someone in it, keep glaring, never see, never find, no end, no matter. He says, no sound, The longer he lives and so the further goes the smaller they grow, the reasoning being the fuller he fills the space and so on, and the emptier, same reasoning. Hell this light from nothing no reason any moment, take off his coat, no, naked, all right, leave it for the moment. Sheets of black paper, stick them to the wall with cobweb and spittle, no good, shine like the rest. Imagine what needed, no more, any given moment, needed no more, gone, never was. Light flows, eyes close, stay closed till it ebbs, no, can't do that, eyes stay open, all right, look at that later. Black bag over his head, no good, all the rest still in light, front, sides, back, between the legs. Black shroud, start search for pins. Light on, down on knees, sights pin, makes for it, light out, gets pin in dark, light on, sights another, light out, so on, years of time on earth. Back on the stool in the shroud saying, That's better, now he's better, and so sits and never stirs, clutching it to him where it gapes, till it all perishes and rots off of him and hangs off of him in black flitters. Light out, long dark, candle and matches, imagine them, strike one to light, light on, blow out, light out,

44

strike another, light on, so on. Light out, strike one to light, light on, light all the same, candlelight in light, blow out, light out, so on. No candle, no matches, no need, never were. As he was, in the dark any length, then the light when it flows till it ebbs any length, then again, so on, sitting, standing, walking, kneeling, crawling, lying, creeping, all any length, no paper, no pins, no candle, no matches, never were, talking to himself no sound in the last person any length, five foot square, six high, all white when light at full, no way in, none out. Falling on his knees in the dark to murmur, no sound, Fancy is his only hope. Surprised by light in this posture, hope and fancy on his lips, crawling lifelong habit to a corner here shadowless and similarly sinking head to ground shining back into his eyes. Imagine eyes burnt ashen blue and lashes gone, lifetime of unseeing glaring, jammed open, one lightning wince per minute on earth, try that. Have him say, no sound. No way in, none out, he's not here. Tighten it round him, three foot square, five high, no stool, no sitting, no kneeling, no lying, just room to stand and revolve, light as before, faces as before, syntaxes upended in opposite corners. The back of his head touches the ceiling, say a lifetime of standing bowed. Call floor angles deasil a, b, c and d and ceiling likewise e, f, g and h, say Jolly at b and Draeger at d, lean him for rest with feet at a and head at g, in dark and light, eyes glaring, murmuring, He's not here, no sound, Fancy is his only hope. Physique, flesh and fell, nail him to that while still tender, nothing clear, place again. Light as before, all white still when at full, flaking plaster or the like, floor like bleached dirt, aha. Faces now naked bodies, eye level, two per wall, eight in all, all right, details later. All six planes hot when shining, aha. So dark and cold any length, shivering more or less, feeble slaps want of room at all flesh within reach, little stamps of hampered feet, so on. Same system light and heat with sweat more or less, cringing away from walls, burning soles, now one, now the other. Murmur unaffected, He's not here, no sound, Fancy dead, gaping eyes unaffected. See how light stops at five soft and mild for bodies, eight no more, one per wall, four in all, say all of Emma. First face alone, lovely beyond words, leave it at that, then deasil breasts alone, then thighs and cunt alone, then arse and hole alone, all lovely beyond words. See how he crouches down and back to see, back of head against face when eyes on cunt, against breasts when on hole, and vice versa, all most clear. So in this soft and mild, crouched down

48

and back with hands on knees to hold himself together, say deasil first from face through hole then back through face, murmuring, imagine him kissing, caressing, licking, sucking, fucking and buggering all this stuff, no sound. Then halt and up to position of rest, back of head touching the ceiling, gaze on ground, lifetime of unbloody bowed unseeing glaring. Imagine lifetime, gems, evenings with Emma and the flights by night, no not that again. Physique, too soon, perhaps never, vague bowed body bonewhite when light at full, nothing clear but ashen glare as imagined, no, attitudes too with play of joints most clear more various now. For nine and nine eighteen that is four feet and more across in which to kneel, arse on heels, hands on thighs, trunk best bowed and crown on ground. And even sit, knees drawn up, trunk best bowed, head between knees, arms round knees to hold all together. And even lie, arse to knees diagonal ac, feet say at d, head on left cheek at b. Price to pay and highest lying more flesh touching glowing ground. But say not glowing enough to burn and turning over, see how that works. Arse to knees, say bd, feet say at c, head on right cheek at a. Then arse to knees say again ac, but feet at b and head on left cheek at d. Then arse to knees say again bd, but feet at a and head on right cheek at c. So on other four possibilities when begin again. All that most clear. Imaginable too flat on back, knees drawn up, hands holding shins to hold all together, glare on ceiling, whereas flat on face by no stretch. Place then most clear so far but of him nothing and perhaps never save jointed segments variously disposed white when light at full. And always there among them somewhere the glaring eyes now clearer still in that flashes of vision few and far now rive their unseeingness. So for example as chance may have it on the ceiling a flyspeck or the insect itself or a strand of Emma's motte. Then lost and all the remaining field for hours of time on earth. Imagination dead imagine to lodge a second in that glare a dying common house or dying window fly, then fall the five feet to the dust and die or die and fall. No, no image, no fly here, no life or dying here but his, a speck of dirt. Or hers since sex not seen so far, say Emma standing, turning, sitting, kneeling, lying, in dark and light, saying to herself, She's not here, no sound, Fancy is her only hope, and Emmo on the walls, first the face, handsome beyond words, then deasil details later. And how crouching down and back she turns murmuring, Fancy her being all kissed, licked, sucked, fucked and so on by all that, no sound, hands on knees to hold herself together. Till halt and up, no, no image, down, for her down, to sit or kneel, kneel, arse on heels, hands on thighs, trunk bowed, breasts hanging, crown on ground, eyes glaring, no, no image, eyes closed, long lashes black when light, no more glare, never was, long black hair strewn when light, murmuring, no sound, Fancy dead. Any length, in dark and light, then topple left, arse to knees say db, feet say at c, head on left cheek at a, left breast puckered in the dust, hands, imagine hands. Imagine hands. Let her lie so from now on, have always lain so, head on left cheek in black hair at a and the rest the only way, never sat, never knelt, never stood, no Emmo, no need, never was. Imagine hands. Left on ball of right shoulder holding enough not to slip, right lightly clenched on ground, something in this hand, imagine later, something soft, clench tight, then lax and still any length, then tight again, so on, imagine later. Highest point from ground top of swell of right haunch, say twenty inches, slim woman. Ceiling wrong now, down two foot, perfect cube now, three foot every way, always was, light as before, all bonewhite when at full as before, floor like bleached dirt, something there, leave it for the moment. Waste height, sixteen inches, strange, say some reason unimaginable now, imagine later, imagination dead imagine all strange away. Jolly and Draeger gone, never were. So far then hollow cube three foot overall, no way in imagined yet, none out. Black cold any length, then light slow up to full glare say ten seconds still and hot glare any length all ivory white all six planes no shadow, then down through deepening greys and gone, so on. Walls and ceiling flaking plaster or such-like, floor like bleached dirt, aha, something there, leave it for the moment. Call floor angles deasil a, b, c and d and in here Emma lying on her left side, arse to knees along diagonal db with arse toward d and knees towards b though neither at either because too short and waste space here too some reason yet to be imagined. On left side then arse to knees db and consequently arse to crown along wall da though not flush because arse out with head on left cheek at a and remaining segment knees to feet along bc not flush because knees out with feet at c. In dark and light. Slow fade of ivory flesh when ebb ten seconds and gone. Long black hair when light strewn over face and adjacent floor. Uncover right eye and cheekbone vivid white for long black lashes when light. Say again though no real image puckered tip of left breast, leave right a mere name. Left hand clinging to right shoulder ball, right more faint loose fist on ground till fingers tighten as though to squeeze, imagine later, then loose again and still any length, so on. Murmuring, no sound, though say lips move with faint stir of hair, whether none emitted or air too rare, Fancy is her only hope, or, She's not here, or, Fancy dead, suggesting moments if discouragement, imagine other murmurs. In dark and light, no, dark alone, say murmurs now in dark alone as though in light all ears all six planes all ears when shining whereas in dark unheard, this a well-known thing. And yet no sound, well say a sound too faint for mortal ear.

Imagine other murmurs. So great
need of words not daring till at last
slow ebb ten seconds, too fast, thirty
now, great need not daring till at last
slow ebb thirty seconds on earth
through a thousand darkening greys
till out and incontinent, Fancy dead,
for instance if spirits low, no sound.
But see how the light dies down and
fron half down or more slow up again
to full and the words down again that
were trembling up, all right, say mere
delay, dark must be in the end, say
dark and light here equal in the end
that is when all done with dead
imagining and measures taken dark
and light seen equal in the end. And
indeed how stay of flow or ebb at any

grey any length and even on the very sill of black any length till at last in and black and at long last the murmur too faint for mortal ear. But murmurs in long dark so long that longing no but need for light as in long light for dark murmurs sometimes as great a space apart as from on earth a winter to a summer day and coming on that great silence, She's not here, for instance if in better spirits or, Fancy is her only hope, too faint for mortal ear. And other times to imagine other extreme so hard on one another any order and sometimes when all spent if not assuaged a second time in some quite different so run together that a mere torrent of hope and unhope mingled and submission amounting to nothing, get all this clearer later. Imagine other murmurs, Mother mother, Mother in heaven, Mother of God, God in heaven, combinations with Christ and Jesus, other proper names in great numbers say of loved ones for the most part and cherished haunts, imagine as needed, un-supported interjections, ancient Greek philosophers ejaculated with place of origin when possible suggesting pursuit of knowledge at some period, completed propositions such as, She is not here, the exception, imagine others, This is not possible, there is one, and here another of exceptional length, In a hammock in the sun and

here the name of some bewitching
site she lies sleeping. But sudden
gleam that whatever words given to
let fall soundless in the dark that if no
sound better none, all right, try sound
and if no better say quite speechless,
imagine sound and not till then all
that black hair toss back into the
corner baring face as about to when
this happened. Quite audible then
now for her and if other ears there
with her in the dark for them and if
ears low down in the wall at a for
them a voice without meaning, hear
that. Then further quite expression-
less, ohs and ahs copulate cold and no
more feeling apparently in hammock
than in Jesus Christ Almighty. And

finally for the moment and then that face the tailaway so common in untrained speakers leaving sometimes in some doubt such things as which Diogenes and what fancy her only. Such then the sound roughly and if no clearer so then all the storm unspoken and the silence unbroken unless sound of light and dark or at the moments of change a sound of flow thirty seconds till full then silence any length till sound of ebb thirty seconds till black then silence any length, that might repay hearing and she hearing open then her eyes to lightening or darkening greys and not close them then to keep them closed till next sound of change till full light or dark, that might well be imagined. But at the same time say here all sound most doubtful though still too soon to deny and that in the end that is when all gone from mind and all mind gone that then none ever been but only silent flesh unless with the faint rise and fall of breast the breath to whip up to a pant if too faint alone and all others denied but still too soon. Hollow cube then three foot overall, full glare, head on left cheek in angle a and the rest the only way and say though no clear image now the long black hair now scattered clear of face on floor so clear when strewn on face now gone some reason, come back to that later, and on the face now bare all

the glare for the moment. Gone the
remembered long black lashes vivid
white so clear before through gap in
hair before all tossed back and lost
some reason and face quite bare suggesting perhaps confusion then with
errant threads of hair itself confused
then with long lashes and so gone with
hair or some other reason now quite
gone. Cease here from face a space to
note how place no longer cube but
rotunda three foot diameter eighteen
inches high supporting a dome semi-
circular in section as in the Pantheon
at Rome or certain beehive tombs and
consequently three foot from ground
to vertex that is at its highest point
no lower than before with loss of

floor space in the neighbourhood of two square feet or six square inches per lost angle and consequences for recumbent readily imaginable and of cubic an even higher figure, all right, resume face. But a, b, c and d now where any pair of right-angled diameters meet circumference meaning tighter fit for Emma with loss if folded as before of nearly one foot from crown to arse and of more than one from arse to knees and of nearly one from knees to feet though she still might be mathematically speaking more than seven foot long and merely a question of refolding in such a way that if head on left cheek at new a and feet at new c then arse no longer at new d but somewhere between it and new c and knees no longer at new b but somewhere between it and new a with segments angled more acutely that is head almost touching knees and feet almost touching arse, all that most clear. Rotunda then three foot diameter and three from ground to vertex, full glare, head on left cheek at a no longer new, when suddenly clear these dimensions faulty and small woman scarce five foot fully extended making rotunda two foot diameter and two from ground to vertex, full glare, face on left cheek at a and long segment that is from crown to arse now necessarily along diagonal too hastily assigned to middle with result face on left cheek with crown against wall at a and no longer feet but *arse* against wall at c there being no alternative and knees against wall ab a few inches from face and feet against wall bc a few inches from arse there being no alternatives and in this way the body tripled or trebled up and wedged in the only possible way in one half of the available room leaving the other empty, aha.

Diagram

Arms and hands as before for the moment. Rotunda then two foot across and at its highest two foot high, full glare, face on left cheek at a, long

67

black hair gone, long black lashes on white cheekbone gone, glare from above for features on this bonewhite undoubted face right profile still hungering for missing lashes burning down for commissure of lids at least when like say without hesitation hell gaping they part and the black eye appears, leave now this face for the moment. Glare now on hands most womanly clear and womanly especially right still loosely clenched as before but no longer on ground since corrected pose but now on outer of right knee just where it swells to thigh while left still loosely hitched to right shoulder ball as before. All that most clear. That black eye still yawning before going down to former to see what all this squeezing note how the other slips a little way down slope of upper arm and then back up to ball, imagine squeeze again. Loose clench any length then crush down most womanly straining knuckles five seconds then back lax any length, all right, now down while fingers loose and in between tips and palm that tiny chink, full glare all this time. No real image but say like red no grey say like something grey and when again squeeze firm down five seconds say faint hiss then silence then back loose two seconds and say faint pop and so arrive though no true image at small grey punctured rubber ball or small grey ordinary rubber bulb such as on earth attached to bottle of scent or suchlike that when squeezed a jet of scent but here alone. So little by little all strange away. Avalanche white lava mud seethe lid over eye permitting return to face of which finally only that it could be nothing else, all right. Thence on to neck in health by nature blank chunk nearer to healthy natural neck with even hint of jugular and cords suggesting perhaps past her best and thence on down to other meat when suddenly when least expected all this prying pointless and enough for the moment and perhaps for ever this place so clear now when light at full and this body hinged and crooked as only the human man or woman living or not when light at full without all this poking and prying about for cracks holes and appendages. Rotunda then as before no change for the moment in dark and light no visible source spread even no shadow slow on thirty seconds to full same off to black two foot high at highest six and a half round good measure, wall peeling plaster or the like supporting dome semi-circular in section same surface, floor bleached dirt or similar, head wedged against wall at a with blank face on left cheek and the rest the only way that is arse wedged against wall at c and knees wedged against wall ab a few inches from face and feet wedged against wall bc a few inches from arse, puckered tip of left breast no real image but maintain for the moment, left hand most clear and womanly lightly clasping right shoulder ball so lightly that slip from time to time down slope of right upper arm then back up to clasp, right no less on upper outer right knee lightly clasping any length small grey rubber sprayer bulb or grey punctured rubber ball then squeeze five seconds on earth faint hiss relax two seconds and pop or not, black right eye like maintain hell gaping any length then seethe of lid to cover imagine frequency later and motive, left also at same time or not or never imagine later, all contained in one hemicycle leaving other vacant, aha. All that if not yet quite complete quite clear and little change likely unless perhaps to complete unless perhaps somehow light sudden gleam perhaps better fixed and all this flowing and ebbing to full and empty more harm than good and soft white unchanging but leave for the moment as seen from outset and never doubted slow on and off thirty seconds to glare and black any length through slow lightening and darkening greys from nothing for no reason yet imagined. Sleep stirring now some time add now with nightmares unimaginable making waking sweet and lying waking till longing for sleep again with dread of demons, perhaps some glimpse of demons later. Dread then in rotunda now with longing and sweet relief but so faint and weak no more than weak tremors of a hot-house leaf. Memories of past felicity no save one faint with faint ripple of sorrow of a lying side by side, look at this closer later. Imagine turning over with help of hinge of neck to bow head towards breast and so temporarily shorten long segment unwedging crown and arse with play enough to writhe till finally head wedged against wall at a as before but on right cheek and arse against wall at c as before but on right cheek and knees against wall a few inches from face as before but wall ad and feet against wall a few inches from arse as before but wall cd and so all tripled up and wedged as before but on the other side to rest the other and within the other hemicycle leaving the other vacant, aha, all that most clear. Clear further how at some earlier more callow stage this writhe again and again in vain through weakness or natural awkwardness or want of pliancy or want of resolution and how halfway through on back with legs just clear how after some time in the balance thus the fall back to where she lay wedged against a wall at a with blank face on left cheek and arse against wall at c and knees against wall ab and feet against wall bc with left hand clutching lightly right shoulder ball and right on upper outer knee small grey sprayer bulb or grey punctured rubber ball with disappointment naturally tinged perhaps with relief and this again and again till final renouncement with faint sweet relief, faint disappointment will have been here too. Sleep if maintained with cacodemons making waking in light and dark if this maintained faint sweet relief and the longing for it again and to be gone again a folly to be resisted again in vain. No memories of felicity save with faint ruffle of sorrow of a lying side by side and of misfortune none, look closer later. So in rotunda up to now with disappointment and relief with dread and longing sorrow all so weak and faint no more than faint tremors of a leaf indoors on earth in winter to survive till spring. Glare back now where all no light immeasurable turmoil no sound black soundless storm of which on earth all being well say one millionth stilled to mean and of that as much again by the more fortunate all being well vented as only humans can. All gone now and never been never still never voiced all back when never sundered unstillable turmoil no sound, She's not here, Fancy is here only, Mother mother, Mother in heaven and of God, God in heaven, Christ and Jesus all combinations, loved ones and places, philosophers and all mere cries, In a hammock etc, and all such, leaving only for the moment, Fancy dead, try that again with spirant barely parting lips in murmur and faint stir of white dust or not in light and dark if this maintained or dark alone as though ears when shining and dead uncertain in dying fall of amateur soliloquy when not known for certain. Last look oh not farewell but last for now on left side tripled up and wedged in half the room head against the wall at a and arse against wall at c and knees against wall ab an inch or so from head and feet against wall bc an inch or so from arse. Then look away then back for left hand clasping lightly right shoulder ball any length till slip and back to clasp and right on upper outer knee any length grey sprayer bulb or small grey punctured rubber ball till squeeze with hiss and loose again with pop or not. Long black hair and lashes gone and puckered breast no details to add to these for the moment save normal neck with hint of cords and jugular and black bottomless eye. Within apart from fancy dead and with faint sorrow faint memory of a lying side by side and in sleep demons not yet imagined all dark unappeasable turmoil no sound and so exhaled only for the moment with faint sound, Fancy dead, to which now add for old mind's sake sorrow vented in simple sighing sound black vowel a and further so that henceforth here no other sounds than these say gone now and never were sprayer bulb or punctured rubber ball and nothing ever in that hand lightly closed on nothing any length till for no reason yet imagined fingers tighten then relax no sound and to the same end slip of left hand down slope of right upper arm no sound and same purpose none of breath to the end that here henceforth no other sounds than these and never were that is than sop to mind faint sighing sound for tremor of sorrow at faint memory of a lying side by side and fancy murmured dead.

PART III

FIVE TEXTS

HEARD IN THE DARK 1

The last time you went out the snow lay on the ground. You now lying in the dark stand that morning on the sill having pulled the door gently to behind you. You lean back against the door with bowed head making ready to set out. By the time you open your eyes your feet have disappeared and the skirts of your greatcoat come to rest on the surface of the snow. The dark scene seems lit from below. You see yourself at that last outset leaning against the door with closed eyes waiting for the word from you to go. You? To be gone. Then the snowlit scene. You lie in the dark with closed eyes and see yourself there as described making ready to strike out and away across the expanse of light. You hear again the clock of the door pulled gently to and the silence before the steps can start. Next thing you are on your way across the white pasture afrolic with lambs in spring and strewn with red placentae. You take the course you always take which is a beeline for the gap or ragged point in the quickset that forms the western fringe. Thither from your entering the pasture you need normally from eighteen hundred to two thousand paces depending on your humour and the state of the ground. But on this last morning many more will be necessary. Many many more. The beeline is so familiar to your feet that if necessary they could keep to it and you sightless with error on arrival of not more than a few feet north or south. And indeed without any such necessity unless from within this is what they normally do and not only here. For you advance if not with closed eyes though this as often as not at least with them fixed on the momentary ground before your feet.

That is all of nature you have seen. Since you finally bowed your head. The fleeting ground before your feet. From time to time. You do not count your steps any more. For the simple reason they number each day the same. Average day in day out the same. The way being always the same. You keep count of the days and every tenth night multiply. And add. Your father's shade is not with you any more. It fell out long ago. You do not hear your footfalls any more. Unhearing unseeing you go your way. Day after day. The same way. As if there were no other any more. For you there is no other any more. You used never to halt except to make your reckoning. So as to plod on from nought anew. This need removed as we have seen there is none in theory to halt any more. Save perhaps a moment at the outermost point. To gather yourself together for the return. And yet you do. As never before. Not for tiredness. You are no more tired now than you always were. Not because of age. You are no older now than you always were. And yet you halt as never before. So that the same hundred yards you used to cover in a matter of three to four minutes may now take you anything from fifteen to twenty. The foot falls unbidden in midstep or next for lift cleaves to the ground bringing the body to a stand. Then a speechlessness whereof the gist, Can they go on? Or better, Shall they go on? The barest gist. Stilled when finally as always hitherto they do. You lie in the dark with closed eyes and see the scene. As you could not at the time. The dark cope of sky. The dazzling land. You at a standstill in the midst. The quarterboots sunk to the tops. The skirts of the greatcoats resting on the snow. In the old bowed head in the old block hat speechless misgiving. Halfway across the pasture on your beeline to the gap. The unerring feet fast. You look behind you as you could not then and see their trail. A great swerve.

Withershins. Almost as if all at once the heart too heavy. In the end too heavy.

HEARD IN THE DARK 2

Bloom of adulthood. Try a whiff of that. On your back in the dark you remember. Ah you remember. Cloudless May day. She joins you in the little summerhouse. Entirely of logs. Both larch and fir. Six feet across. Eight from floor to vertex. Area twenty-four square feet to the furthest decimal. Two small multicoloured lights vis-à-vis. Small stained diamond panes. Under each a ledge. There on summer Sundays after his midday meal your father loved to retreat with Punch and a cushion. The waist of his trousers unbuttoned he sat on the one ledge and turned the pages. You on the other your feet dangling. When he chuckled you tried to chuckle too. When his chuckle died yours too. That you should try to imitate his chuckle pleased and amused him greatly and sometimes he would chuckle for no other reason than to hear you try to chuckle too. Sometimes you turn your head and look out through a rose-red pane. You press your little nose against the pane and all without is rosy. The years have flown and there at the same place as then you sit in the bloom of adulthood bathed in rainbow light gazing before you. She is late. You close your eyes and try to calculate the volume. Simple sums you find a help in times of trouble. A haven. You arrive in the end at seven cubic yards approximately. Even still in the timeless dark you find figures a comfort. You assume a certain heart rate and reckon how many thumps a day. A week. A month. A year. And assuming a certain lifetime a lifetime. Till the last thump. But for the moment with hardly more than seventy American billion behind you you sit in the little summerhouse working out the volume. Seven cubic yards approximately. This strikes you for some reason as improbable and you set about your sum anew. But you have not got very far when her light step is heard. Light for a woman of her size. You open with quickening pulse your eyes and a moment later that seems an eternity her face appears at the window. Mainly blue in this position the natural pallor you so admire as indeed from it no doubt wholly blue your own. For natural pallow is a property you have in common. The violet lips do not return your smile. Now this window being flush with your eyes from where you sit and the floor as near as no matter with the outer ground you cannot but wonder if she has not sunk to her knees. Knowing from experience that the height or length you have in common is the sum of equal segments. For when bolt upright or lying at full stretch you cleave front to front then your knees touch and your pubes and the hairs of your heads mingle. Does it follow from this that the loss of height for the body that sits is the same as for it that kneels? At this point assuming level of seat adjustable as in the case of certain piano stools you close your eyes the better with mental measure to measure and compare the first and second segments namely from sole to kneepad and thence to pelvic girdle. How given you were both moving and at rest to the closed eye in your waking hours! By day and by night. To that perfect dark. That shadowless light. Simply to be gone. Or for affair as now. A single leg appears. Seen from above. You separate the segments and lay them side by side. It is as you half surmised. The upper is the longer and the sitter's loss the greater when seat at knee level. You leave the pieces lying there and open your eyes to find her sitting before you. All dead still. The ruby lips do not return your smile. Your gaze moves down to the breasts. You do not remember them so big. To the abdomen. Same impression. Dissolve to your father's straining against the unbuttoned waistband. Can it be she is with child without your having asked for as much as her hand? You go back into your mind. She too did you but know it has closed her eyes. So you sit face to face in the little summerhouse. With eyes closed and hands on knees. In the bloom of your adulthood. In that rainbow light. That dead still.

ONE EVENING

He was found lying on the ground. No one had missed him. No one was looking for him. An old woman found him. To put it vaguely. It happened so long ago. She was straying in search of wild flowers. Yellow only. With no eyes but for these she stumbled on him lying there. He lay face downward and arms outspread. He wore a greatcoat

in spite of the time of year. Hidden
by the body a long row of buttons
fastened it all the way down. Buttons
of all shapes and sizes. Worn upright
the skirts swept the ground. At once
on its brim and crown. He lay
inconspicuous in the greenish coat.
To catch an eye searching from afar
there was only the white head. May
she have seen him somewhere
before? Somewhere on his feet
before? Not too fast. She was all in
black. The hem of her long black
skirt trailed in the grass. It was close
of day. Should she now move away
into the east her shadow would go
before. A long black shadow. It was
lambing time. But there were no

lambs. She could see none. Were a third party to chance that way theirs were the only bodies he would see. First that of the old woman standing. Then on drawing near it lying on the ground. That seems to hang together. The deserted fields. The old woman all in black stockstill. The body stockstill on the ground. Yellow at the end of the black arm. The white hair in the grass. The east foundering in night. Not too fast. The weather. Sky overcast all day till evening. In the west-north-west near the verge already the sun came out at last. Rain? A few drops if you will. A few drops in the morning if you will. In the present to conclude. It happened so long ago. Cooped indoors all day she comes out with the sun. She makes haste to gain the fields. Surprised to have seen no one on the way she strays feverishly in search of the wild flowers. Feverishly seeing the imminence of night. She remarks with surprise the absence of lambs in great numbers here at this time of year. She is wearing the black she took on when widowed young. It is to reflower the grave she strays in search of the flowers he had loved. But for the need of yellow at the end of the black arm there would be none. There are therefore only as few as possible. This is for her the third surprise since she came out. For they grow in plenty here at this time of year. Her old friend her shadow irks her. So much so that she turns to face the sun. Any flower wide of her course she reaches sidelong. She craves for sundown to end and to stray freely again in the long afterglow. Further to her distress the familiar rustle of her long black skirt in the grass. She moves with half-closed eyes as if drawn on into the glare. She may say to herself it is too much strangeness for a single March or April evening. No one abroad. Not a single lamb. Scarcely a flower. Shadow and rustle irksome. And to crown all the shock of her foot against a body. Chance. No one had missed him. No one was looking for him. Black and green of the garments touching now. Near the white head the yellow of the few plucked flowers. The old sunlit face. Tableau vivant if you will. In its way. All is silent from now on. For as long as she cannot move. The sun disappears at last and with it all shadow. All shadow here. Slow fade of afterglow. Night without moon or stars. All that seems to hang together. But no more about it.

AS THE
STORY WAS TOLD

As the story was told me I never went near the place during sessions. I asked what place and a tent was described at length, a small tent the colour of its surroundings. Wearying of this description I asked what sessions and these in turn were described, their object, duration, frequency and harrowing nature. I hope I was not

103

more sensitive than the next man, but finally I had to raise my hand. I lay there quite still for a time, then asked where I was while all this was going forward. In a hut, was the asnwer, a small hut in a grove some two hundred yards away, a distance even the loudest cry could not carry, but must die on the way. This was not so strange as at first sight it sounded when one considered the stoutness of the canvas and the sheltered situation of the hut among the trees. Indeed the tent might have been struck where it stood and moved forward fifty yards or so without inconvenience. Lying there with closed eyes in the silence which

followed this information I began to
see the hut, though unlike the tent it
had not been described to me, but
only its situation. It reminded me
strongly of a summer-house in which
as a child I used to sit quite still for
hours on end, on the window-seat,
the whole year round. It had the same
five log walls, the same coloured
glass, the same diminutiveness, being
not more than ten feet across and so
low of ceiling that the average man
could not have held himself erect in
it, though of course there was no
such difficulty for the child. At the
centre, facing the coloured panes,
stood a small upright wicker chair
with arm-rests, as against the

summer-house's window-seat. I sat there very straight and still, with my arms along the rests, looking out at the orange light. It must have been shortly after six, the sessions closing punctually at that hour, for as I watched a hand appeared in the doorway and held out to me a sheet of writing. I took and read it, then tore it in four and put the pieces in the waiting hand to take away. A little later the whole scene disappeared. As the story was told me the man succumbed in the end to his ill-treatment, though quite old enough at the time to die naturally of old age. I lay there a long time quite still — even as a child I was unusually

still and more and more so with the
passing years — till it must have
seemed the story was over. But
finally I asked if I knew exactly what
the man — I would like to give his
name but cannot — what exactly was
required of the man, what it was he
would not or could not say. No, was
the answer, after some little hesitation no, I did not know what the
poor man was required to say, in
order to be pardoned, but would
have recognized it at once, yes, at a
glance, if I had seen it.

NEITHER

to and fro in shadow from inner to
outershadow

from impenetrable self to impenetrable unself by way of neither

as between two lit refuges whose
doors once? gently close, once turned
away from gently part again

beckoned back and forth and turned
away

heedless of the way, intent on the one
gleam or the other

unheard footfalls only sound

till at last halt for good, absent for
good from self and other

then no sound

then gently light unfading on that
unheeded neither

unspeakable home

Written for the composer Morton Feldman, 1962

PART IV

STIRRINGS STILL

STIRRINGS STILL

I

One night as he sat at his table head on hands he saw himself rise and go. One night or day. For when his own light went out he was not left in the dark. Light of a kind came then from the one high window. Under it still the stool on which till he could or would no more he used to mount to

113

see the sky. Why he did not crane out to see what lay beneath was perhaps because the window was not made to open or because he could or would not open it. Perhaps he knew only too well what lay beneath and did not wish to see it again. So he would simply stand there high above the earth and see through the clouded pane the cloudless sky. Its faint unchanging light unlike any light he could remember from the days and nights when day followed hard on night and night on day. This outer light then when his own went out became his only light till it in its turn went out and left him in the dark. Till it in its turn went out.

One night or day then as he sat at his table head on hands he saw himself rise and go. First rise and stand clinging to the table. Then sit again. Then rise again and stand clinging to the table again. Then go. Start to go. On unseen feet start to go. So slow that only change of place to show he went. As when he disappeared only to reappear later at another place. Then disappeared again only to reappear again later at another place again. So again and again disappeared again only to reappear again at another place again. Another place in the place where he sat at his table head on hands. The same place and table as when Darly for example died

115

and left him. As when others too in their turn before and since. As when others would too in their turn and leave him till he too in his turn. Head on hands half hoping when he disappeared again that he would not reappear again and half fearing that he would not. Or merely wondering. Or merely waiting. Waiting to see if he would or would not. Leave him or not alone again waiting for nothing again.

Seen always from behind whithersoever he went. Same hat and coat as of old when he walked the roads. The back roads. Now as one in a strange place seeking the way out. In the dark. In a strange place blindly in the dark of night or day seeking the way out. A way out. To the roads. The back roads.

A clock afar struck the hours and half-hours. The same as when among others Darly once died and left him. Strokes now clear as if carried by a wind now faint on the still air. Cries afar now faint now clear. Head on hands half hoping when the hour struck that the half-hour would not and half fearing that it would not. Similarly when the half-hour struck. Similarly when the cries a moment ceased. Or merely wondering. Or merely waiting. Waiting to hear.

There had been a time he would sometimes lift his head enough to see his hands. What of them was to be seen. One laid on the table and the other on the one. At rest after all they did. Lift his past head a moment to see his past hands. Then lay it back on them to rest it too. After all it did.

The same place as when left day after day for the roads. The back roads. Returned to night after night. Paced from wall to wall in the dark. The then fleeting dark of night. Now as if strange to him seen to rise and go. Disappear and reappear at another place. Disappear again and reappear again at another place again. Or at the same. Nothing to show not the same. No wall toward which or from. No table back toward which or further from. In the same place as when paced from wall to wall all places as the same. Or in another. Nothing to show not another. Where never. Rise and go in the same place as ever. Disappear and reappear in another where never. Nothing to show not another where never. Nothing but the strokes. The cries. The same as ever.

Till so many strokes and cries since he was last seen that perhaps he would not be seen again. Then so many cries since the strokes were last heard that perhaps they would not be heard again. Then such silence since the cries were last heard that perhaps even they would not be heard again.

Perhaps thus the end. Unless no more than a mere lull. Then all as before. The strokes and cries as before and he as before now there now gone now there again now gone again. Then the lull again. Then all as before again. So again and again. And patience till the one true end to time and grief and self and second self his own.

2

As one in his right mind when at last out again he knew not how he was not long out again when he began to wonder if he was in his right mind. For could one not in his right mind be reasonably said to wonder if he was in his right mind and bring what is more his remains of reason to bear on this perplexity in the way he must be said to do if he is to be said at all? It was therefore in the guise of a more or less reasonable being that he emerged at last he knew not how into the outer world and had not been there for more than six or seven hours by the clock when he could not but begin to wonder if he was in his right mind. By the same clock whose strokes were those heard times without number in his confinement as it struck the hours and half hours and so in a sense at first a source of reassurance till finally one of alarm as being no clearer now than when in principle muffled by his four walls. Then he sought help in the thought of one hastening westward at sundown to obtain a better view of Venus and found it of none. Of the sole other sound that of cries enlivener of his solitude as lost to suffering he sat at his table head on hands the same was true. Of their whereabouts that is of clock and cries the same was true that is no more to be determined now than as was only natural then. Bringing to bear on all this his remains of reason he sought help in the thought that his memory of indoors was perhaps at fault and found it of none. Further to his disarray his soundless tread as when barefoot he trod his floor. So all ears from bad to worse till in the end he ceased if not to hear to listen and set out to look about him. Result finally he was in a field of grass which went some way if nothing else to explain his tread and then a little later as if to make up for this some way to increase his trouble. For he could recall no field of grass from even the very heart of which no limit of any kind was to be discovered but always in some quarter or another some end in sight such as a fence or other manner of bourne from which to return. Nor on his looking more closely to make matters worse was this the short green grass he seemed to remember eaten down by flocks and herds but long and light grey in colour verging here and there on white. Then he sought help in the thought that his memory of outdoors was perhaps at fault and found it of none. So all eyes from bad to worse till in the end he ceased if not to see to look (about him or more closely) and set out to take thought. To this end for want of a stone on which to sit like Walther and cross his legs the best he could do was stop dead and stand stock still which after a moment of hesitation he did and of course sink his head as one deep in meditation which after another moment of hesitation he did also. But soon weary of vainly delving in those remains he moved on through the long hoar grass resigned to not knowing where he was or how he got there or where he was going or how to get back to whence he knew not how he came. So on unknowing and no end in sight. Unknowing and what is more no wish to know nor indeed any wish of any kind nor therefore any sorrow save that he would have wished the strokes to cease and the cries for good and was sorry that they did not. The strokes now faint now clear as if carried by the wind but not a breath and the cries now faint now clear.

3

So on till stayed when to his ears from deep within oh how and here a word he could not catch it were to end where never till then. Rest then before again from not long to so long that perhaps never again and then again faint from deep within oh how and here that missing word again it were to end where never till then. In any case whatever it might be to end and so on was he not already as he stood there all bowed down to his ears faint from deep within again and again oh how something and so on was he not so far as he could see already there where never till then?

For how could even such a one as he having once found himself in such a place not shudder to find himself in it again which he had not done nor having shuddered seek help in vain in the thought so-called that having somehow got out of it then he could somehow get out of it again which he had not done either. There then all this time where never till then and so far as he could see in every direction when he raised his head and opened his eyes no danger or hope as the case might be of his ever getting out of it. Was he then now to press on regard- less now in one direction and now in another or on the other hand stir no more as the case might be that is as that missing word might be which if to warn such as sad or bad for example then of course in spite of all the one and if the reverse then of course the other that is stir no more. Such and much more such the hubbub in his mind so-called till nothing left from deep within but only ever fainter oh to end. No matter how no matter where. Time and grief and self so-called. Oh all to end.

PART V

WHAT IS THE WORD

WHAT IS THE WORD

folly —
folly for to —
for to —
what is the word —
folly from this —
all this —
folly from all this —
given —
folly given all this —
seeing —

folly seeing all this —
this —
what is the word —
this this —
this this here —
all this this here —
folly given all this —
seeing —
folly seeing all this this here —
for to —
what is the word —
see —
glimpse —
seem to glimpse —
need to seem to glimpse —
folly for to need to seem to glimpse —
what —
what is the word —

and where —
folly for to need to seem to glimpse
                              what where —
where —
what is the word —
there —
over there —
away over there —
afar —
afar away over there —
afaint —
afaint afar away over there what —
what —
what is the word —
seeing all this —
all this this —
all this this here —
folly for to see what —

glimpse —
seem to glimpse —
need to seem to glimpse —
afaint afar away over there what —
folly for to need to seem to glimpse
   afaint afar away over there what —
what —
what is the word —

what is the word